NO LONGER P
Seattle Public Library
D0395424

GRAND TRIAL SHOWDOWN

2 GRAPHIC ADVENTURES

Adapted by
Simcha Whitehill

Scholastic Inc.

©2019 Pokémon. ©1997–2019 Nintendo, Creatures, GAME FREAK, TV Tokyo, ShoPro, JR Kikaku. TM, ®Nintendo.

All rights reserved. Published by Scholastic Inc., *Publishers since 1920.* SCHOLASTIC and associated logos are trademarks and/or registered trademarks of Scholastic Inc.

The publisher does not have any control over and does not assume any responsibility for author or third-party websites or their content.

No part of this publication may be reproduced, stored in a retrieval system, or transmitted in any form or by any means, electronic, mechanical, photocopying, recording, or otherwise, without written permission of the publisher. For information regarding permission, write to Scholastic Inc., Attention: Permissions Department, 557 Broadway, New York, NY 10012.

This book is a work of fiction. Names, characters, places, and incidents are either the product of the author's imagination or are used fictitiously, and any resemblance to actual persons, living or dead, business establishments, events, or locales is entirely coincidental.

ISBN 978-1-338-56889-9

10 9 8 7 6 5 4 3 2 1 19 20 21 22 23

Printed in China 38
First printing 2019

Book design by DeMonico Design, Co.

CONTENTS

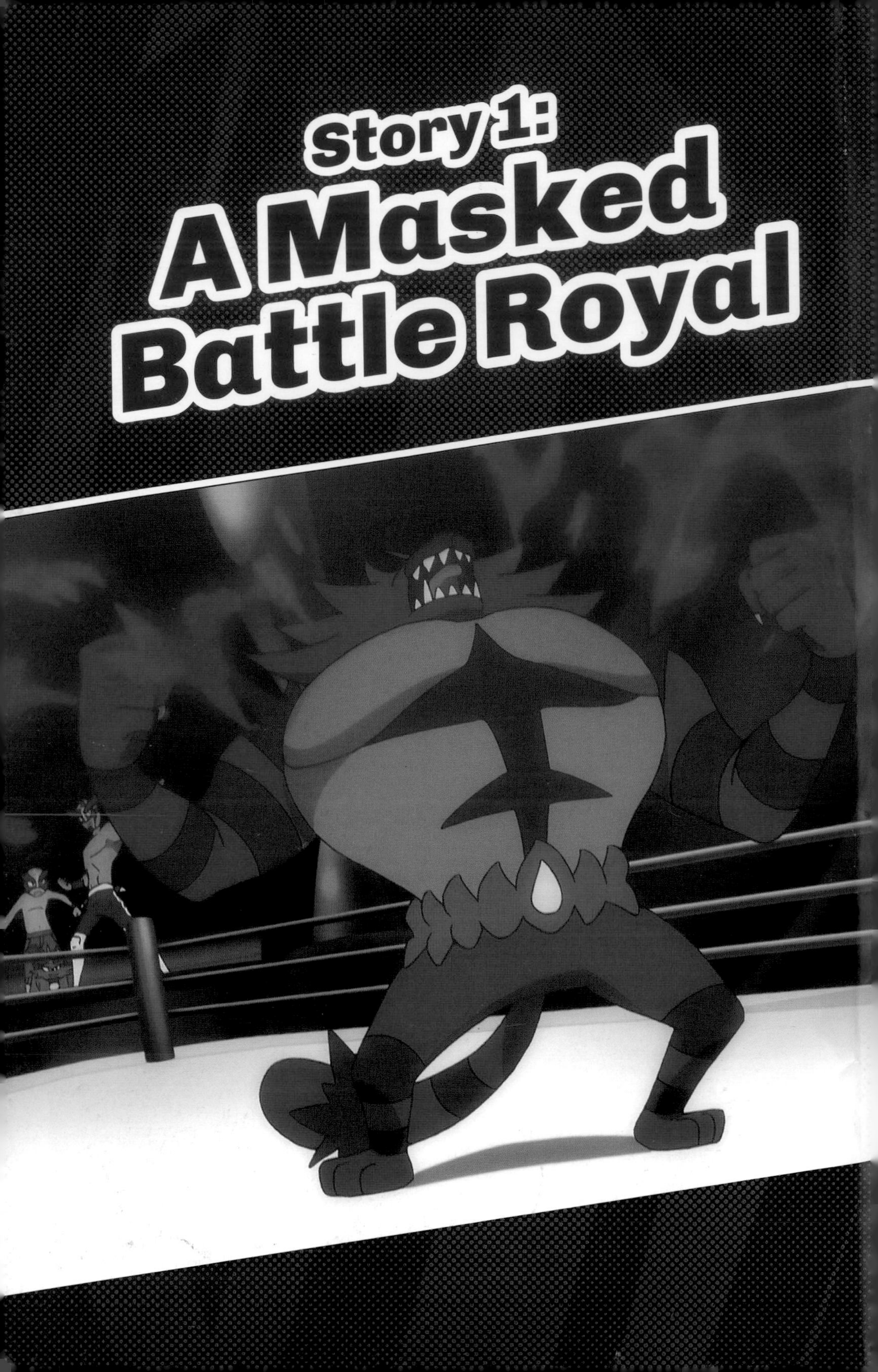
Story 1:
A Masked
Battle Royal

ASH AND HIS FRIENDS WERE WATCHING A NEW EPISODE OF THEIR FAVORITE TELEVISION SHOW: *THE BATTLE ROYAL*. IT FEATURED EPIC BATTLES BETWEEN TOP TRAINERS AND THEIR POKÉMON AT THE BATTLE ROYAL DOME.

THE TOUGHEST TEAM OUT THERE IN THE RING WAS THE STARS OF THE SHOW—THE MASKED ROYAL AND HIS POKÉMON PARTNER, INCINEROAR.

No one knew the true identity of the Masked Royal, but he had real enemies. There was a crew of trainers who wanted to take him down—the Revengers.
In this episode, the Masked Royal faced two of his Revenger rivals: Mr. Electric and Electivire.
EEEELECTIVIIIRE!
The crowd cheered for the Masked Royal and Incineroar as they took the stage. They began the battle with a direct hit.
INCINEROAR, USE CROSS CHOP!
RRRRROOAR!
Then, Mr. Electric sneaked up to the ring to pull one of his pranks.
IIIIRRRRE?!
IT NOW APPEARS THAT MR. ELECTRIC HAS GRABBED INCINEROAR'S LEG!

GASP!
ELECTIVIRE'S SET TO CLOBBER INCINEROAR FROM BEHIND!
THE MASKED ROYAL THOUGHT FAST AND CALLED OUT TO HIS AMBUSHED BUDDY.
NOW, USE THROAT CHOP!

INCINEROAR WAS ABOUT TO STRIKE BACK . . .
RRRRRRRRRROAR!
POW!
WHEN IT TOOK A SURPRISE BLOW TO THE BACK FROM TWO MORE REVENGERS.
IT SEEMS THE TEAM OF MAD MAGMA AND MAGMORTAR HAS RUSHED IN!
HA HA HA HA HA!
BOO!
A BELL RANG, CALLING THE MATCH.
ROTOM DEX, WHAT JUST HAPPENED?
MAGMORTAR HAD NO RIGHT TO ENTER THE RING, SO THE TEAM OF MR. ELECTRIC AND ELECTIVIRE IS DISQUALIFIED.
I'M SURE THE MASKED ROYAL DIDN'T WANT TO WIN THE MATCH LIKE THAT . . .

THEN, MAD MAGMA MADE HIS DEMANDS.
NOW LISTEN UP, MASKED ROYAL! IF YOU REALLY HAD GUTS, YOU'D HAVE A ONE-ON-ONE BATTLE WITH ME TO PROVE WHO'S THE STRONGEST AT THE BATTLE ROYAL DOME!
ALL RIGHT THEN. I ACCEPT!
WE'LL HAVE OUR MAIN EVENT SHOWDOWN . . . TOMORROW!
INCINEROAR WAS EXCITED AT THE CHANCE TO TAKE ON THOSE REVENGER CHUMPS.
RRRRRRRRROAR!

THE BATTLE WOULD BE DIFFICULT, BUT THE TOUGHEST PART FOR THE MASKED ROYAL WOULD BE KEEPING HIS IDENTITY A SECRET. HE'S PROFESSOR KUKUI, AND HE HAD BEEN HIDING HIS ALTER EGO FROM HIS WIFE, PROFESSOR BURNET, AND ASH!
JOIN US, KUKUI! TWO, THREE . . .
ENNNNJOY!
WOW! WELL, YOU'VE BEEN PRACTICING, HAVEN'T YOU?

UH . . . PRACTICING?! GUILTY AS CHARGED! HA HA . . .
WE'RE ALL GOING TOGETHER TO SEE THE MATCH TOMORROW AT THE BATTLE ROYAL DOME!
AND YOU'RE COMING, TOO!
EVERYBODY FROM SCHOOL IS COMING, TOO!
I'M COMING?!
UH. ARE YOU BUSY?
HA HA . . . UH, IT'LL BE GREAT FUN!
THE NEXT DAY, THEY ALL MADE THEIR WAY TO THE BATTLE ROYAL DOME. EVERYONE IN THE STADIUM WAS THRILLED TO HAVE TICKETS TO SEE THIS SPECIAL BATTLE LIVE—WELL, EXCEPT PROFESSOR KUKUI.
IT'S REALLY GREAT TO BE SEEING THIS WITH ALL MY BUDDIES!
I'M SO PUMPED UP; I FEEL LIKE I COULD BURST!
GULP!

WHEN IT WAS ALMOST TIME FOR THE MATCH, PROFESSOR KUKUI TRIED TO SNEAK OUT.
HOLD ON . . . WHERE ARE YOU GOING?
UH . . . JUST FOR A QUICK SNACK RUN! I'LL GO U-TURN AND BE BACK IN NO TIME FLAT!
SOON, THE LIGHTS CAME UP ON THE RING. THE STAGE WAS SET.
THE BATTLE ROYAL DOME POWERFEST! AND FIRST, I INTRODUCE MAGMORTAR AND MAD MAGMA!
MAGMORTAR!
HA HA HA HA HA!
AND OVER HERE, IT'S INCINEROAR AND THE MASKED ROYAL!
ENNNNJOY!

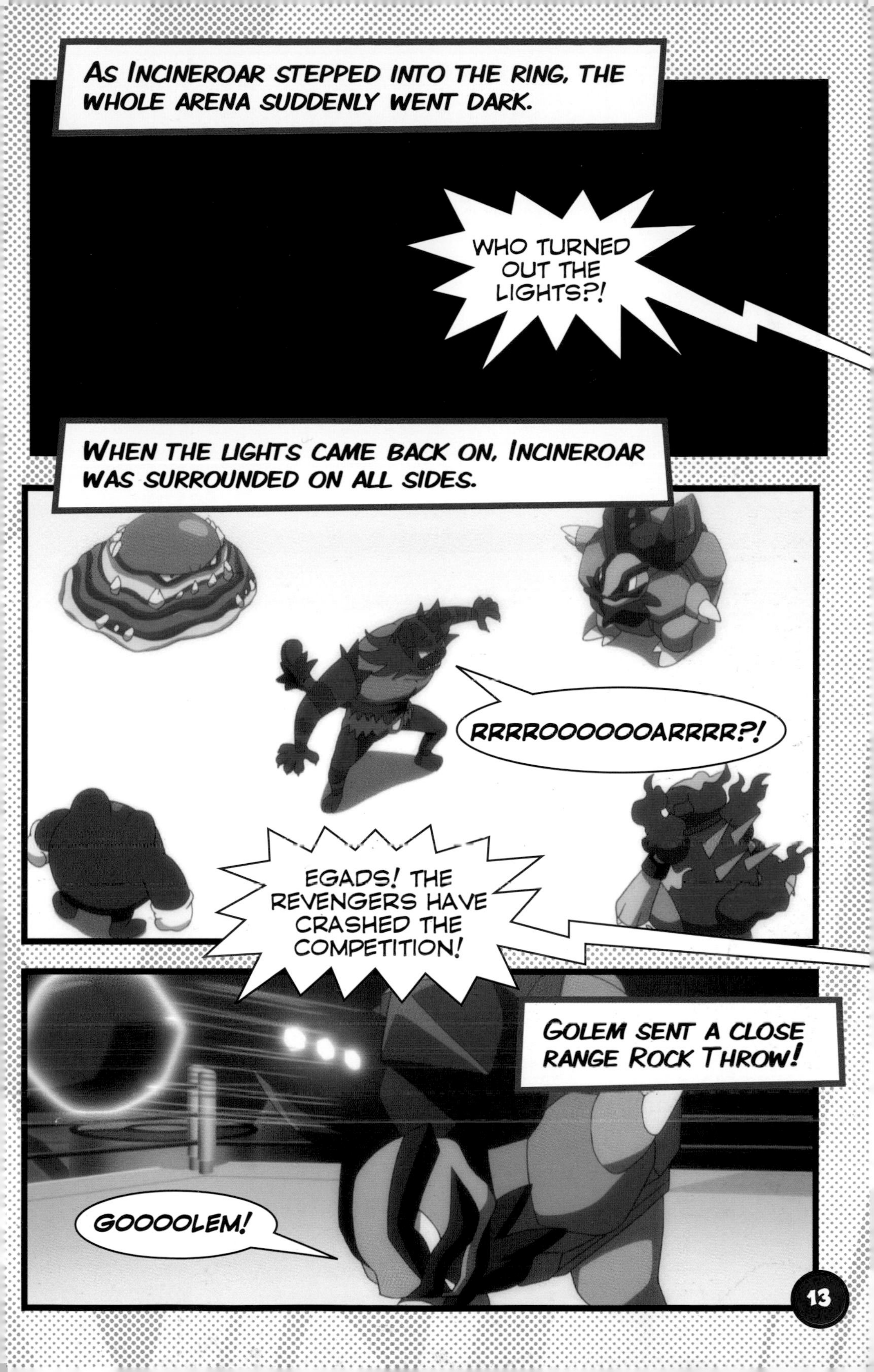
As Incineroar stepped into the ring, the whole arena suddenly went dark.
WHO TURNED OUT THE LIGHTS?!
When the lights came back on, Incineroar was surrounded on all sides.
RRRROOOOOOOARRRR?!
EGADS! THE REVENGERS HAVE CRASHED THE COMPETITION!
Golem sent a close range Rock Throw!
GOOOOLEM!

POLIWRATH BLASTED A POWERFUL WATER GUN!
WRRRRRRRATH!
MAGMORTAR FIRED A TERRIBLE FLAMETHROWER!
MAAAAAAAGMORTAAAAR!
MUK SHOT A SLIMY ACID SPRAY!
UUUUUUUUGHCK!

THEN, GOLEM, POLIWRATH, AND MUK PINNED INCINEROAR DOWN. MAGMORTAR CLIMBED UP ON THE CORNER, PREPARING ITS INFAMOUS FIRE PUNCH.

RRRRRRRRROOOOOAR . . .

BUT BEFORE IT COULD JUMP, TORRACAT FLEW DOWN FROM THE STAND WITH A FIERCE FLAME CHARGE TO PROTECT INCINEROAR . . .

TWO-FOOT TALL TORRACAT IS SO TOUGH, IT WAS ABLE TO PUSH MASSIVE MAGMORTAR OFF ITS PERCH.

THE CROWD CHEERED FOR TORRACAT'S BRAVERY. ASH FOLLOWED HIS FRIEND DOWN TO THE RING TO OFFICIALLY OFFER HELP TO THEIR HERO, THE MASKED ROYAL.
APPLAUSE!
WOO-HOO!
ALL RIGHT, TORRACAT!
TORRACAT!
YEAH!
UNFORTUNATELY, MORE FIGHTERS ALSO ARRIVED IN THE RING—THE REST OF THE REVENGERS. THEIR LEADER GOT ON THE MIC TO MAKE ANOTHER CHALLENGE.
THE NAME IS VIREN. I'M THE PROUD PRESIDENT OF RAINBOW HAPPY RESORTS, AND I RUN THE REVENGERS FROM THE SHADOWS—BECAUSE I'M THE BIG BOSS!
ASH RECOGNIZED VIREN—HE WAS THE GUY WHO TRIED TO DESTROY HIS FRIEND KIAWE'S FARM.
GASP! THE BIG BOSS?!

TODAY, THE REVENGERS WILL PROVE THEMSELVES AS THE BEST OF THE BATTLE ROYAL DOME! THEN WE'LL BUY THE JOINT! WE'LL TURN IT INTO A SUBSIDIARY OF THE RAINBOW HAPPY RESORTS! HA HA HA!
FORGET IT!
WE DEMAND A REVENGE GRUDGE MATCH, HERE AND NOW! WHY DON'T YOU TEAM UP FOR A TAG-TEAM MATCH WITH THAT TORRACAT AND ITS TRAINER, BATTLING AGAINST THE REVENGERS FOR THE PRESTIGE OF THE STRONGEST ON THE LINE?
TORRACAT WAS NOT AFRAID OF THOSE TRASH-TALKING BULLIES!
TORRRRRRRRRR!

WE'RE NOT RUNNING AWAY! RIGHT, MASKED ROYAL?
YOU MEAN IT? YOU AND US? WE'LL BATTLE THE REVENGERS TOGETHER?
OF COURSE WE WILL! WON'T WE, TORRACAT?!
TORRACAT!
WE ACCEPT YOUR CHALLENGE!
THE CROWD WENT WILD—INCLUDING ASH'S PROUD FRIENDS UP IN THE BLEACHERS!

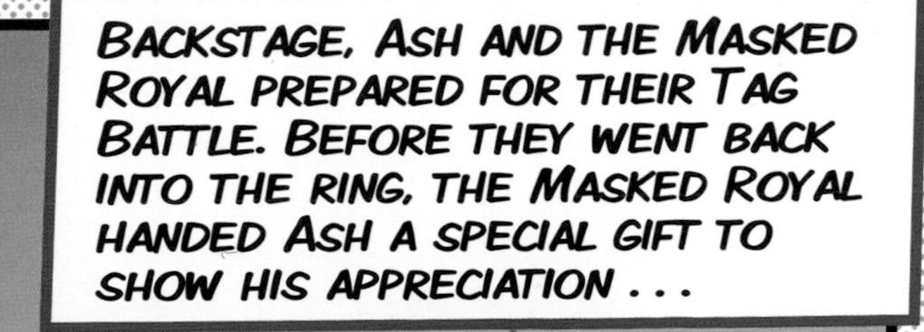
BACKSTAGE, ASH AND THE MASKED ROYAL PREPARED FOR THEIR TAG BATTLE. BEFORE THEY WENT BACK INTO THE RING, THE MASKED ROYAL HANDED ASH A SPECIAL GIFT TO SHOW HIS APPRECIATION . . .
THAT MASK IS FOR ME? NO WAY!
YES WAY! YOU ARE NOW KNOWN AS ASH ROYAL!
WOW! MY NAME IS ASH ROYAL!
ASH SLIPPED ON THE MASK AND FOLLOWED HIS HERO ONTO THE STAGE!

WE PRESENT THE DUO OF THE MASKED ROYAL AND ASH ROYAL, SO LET'S GIVE THE DOUBLE ROYALS A BIG HAND!
ENNNNJOY!

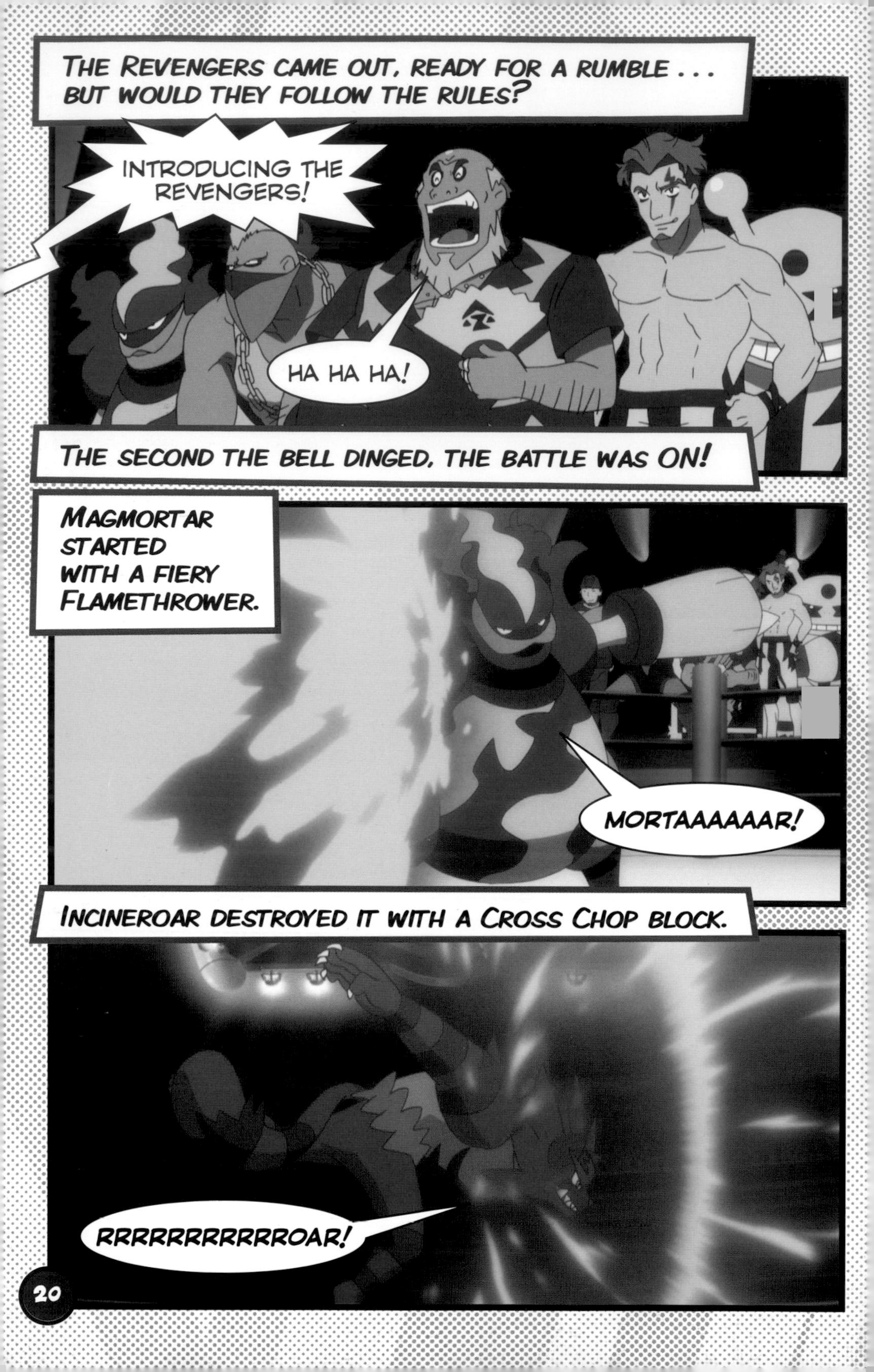
THE REVENGERS CAME OUT, READY FOR A RUMBLE . . . BUT WOULD THEY FOLLOW THE RULES?
INTRODUCING THE REVENGERS!
HA HA HA!
THE SECOND THE BELL DINGED, THE BATTLE WAS ON!
MAGMORTAR STARTED WITH A FIERY FLAMETHROWER.
MORTAAAAAAR!
INCINEROAR DESTROYED IT WITH A CROSS CHOP BLOCK.
RRRRRRRRRRROAR!

NOW IN CLOSE RANGE COMBAT, MAGMORTAR KNOCKED OUT A KARATE CHOP, AND INCINEROAR THREW A THROAT CHOP PUNCH.
RRROOOOOAAAAAARRRRRR!
MORTAAAARRRRRRR!
THEIR ATTACKS APPEARED TO BE CANCELING EACH OTHER OUT.
SO THE DOUBLE ROYALS DECIDED TO SWITCH, AND TORRACAT TAPPED IN FOR INCINEROAR.
MAD MAGMA WAS READY FOR HIS CHANCE TO GET REVENGE . . .
YOU'RE THE ONE WHO HIT MAGMORTAR OUT OF NOWHERE, AREN'T YOU?
BECAUSE YOU BROKE THE RULES IN THE FIRST PLACE!
MAD MAGMA HAD MAGMORTAR START OFF ON ITS TIPTOES WITH A TRICKY FEINT . . .
AND TORRACAT FELL RIGHT FOR IT.

MAGMORTAR GRABBED TORRACAT, TWIRLED IT IN THE AIR, AND TOSSED IT.
AAAAH–AAAAAH–AAAAAAAT!
AMAZINGLY, TORRACAT LANDED ON ITS FEET!
BUT WHEN IT WENT TO RESPOND WITH SCRATCH, TORRACAT DISCOVERED ITS TAIL HAD BEEN SNATCHED BY POLIWHIRL.
HEY, THAT'S NOT FAIR!

ONLY THE WINNERS MAKE THE RULES!
THEN, MR. ELECTRIC AND ELECTIVIRE STEPPED INTO THE RING FOR THE REVENGERS.
ELECTIVIRE!
CAAAAAAAAAAAAAAAT!
ELECTIVI-I-I-I-I!

THEN, TORRACAT TRADED PLACES WITH ITS TEAMMATE INCINEROAR.

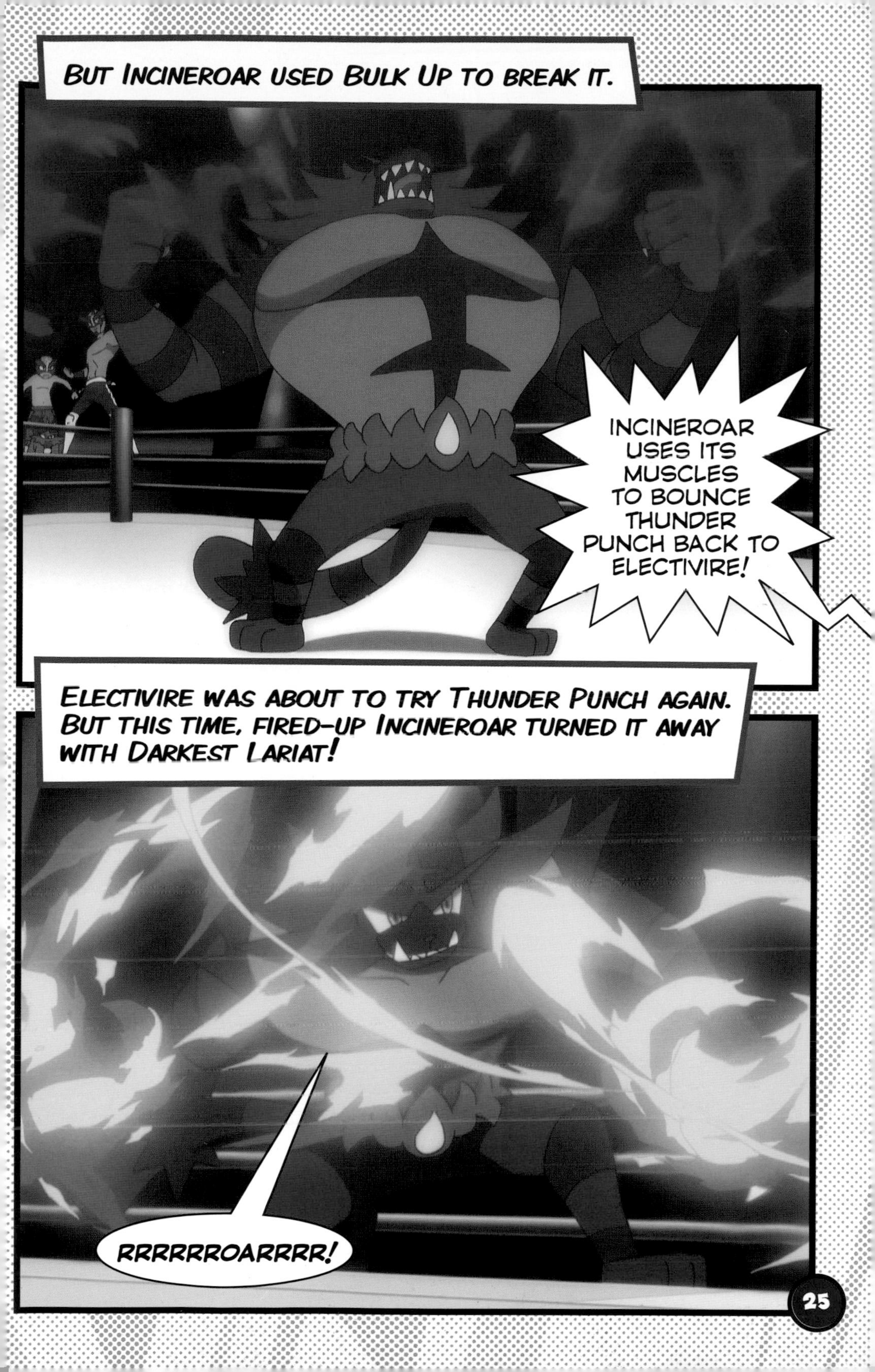

BUT INCINEROAR USED BULK UP TO BREAK IT.
INCINEROAR USES ITS MUSCLES TO BOUNCE THUNDER PUNCH BACK TO ELECTIVIRE!
ELECTIVIRE WAS ABOUT TO TRY THUNDER PUNCH AGAIN. BUT THIS TIME, FIRED-UP INCINEROAR TURNED IT AWAY WITH DARKEST LARIAT!
RRRRRROARRRR!

VIIIIIRE!
WHOOOSH!

BEFORE INCINEROAR COULD MAKE ITS NEXT MOVE, IT WAS PULLED IN ANOTHER DIRECTION BY THE CHEATING REVENGERS.
ROARRRRRRR?

THE FANS IN THE STANDS WERE IN AN UPROAR!
IT ISN'T FAIR!
BOO!
THAT'S IT!
SO THEY DECIDED TO ASK THEIR POKÉMON PALS TO STEP IN . . .
KIAWE ASKED MAROWAK TO DIVE IN WITH IRON HEAD.
MAAAAROOOOO!
LANA CALLED ON POPPLIO TO STREAM IN WITH AQUA JET.
PAAAAAAAAAAAH!
THE MASKED ROYAL ASKED HIS BRAVE SUPPORTERS TO RETURN TO THEIR SEATS. HE WAS TOUCHED BY THEIR SUPPORT, BUT HE WANTED TO PLAY BY THE RULES.

IT WAS TIME TO SWITCH IT UP! INCINEROAR AND ELECTIVIRE TAGGED OUT. TORRACAT AND MAGMORTAR TOOK TO THE RING.

EE-EEE-ELECTIVIRE.

THE BATTLE GOT EVEN MORE HEATED.

TORRACAAAAAAAAAAT!

TORRACAT LAUNCHES LIKE A MISSILE FROM THE TOP OF THE POST AND DELIVERS A BLAZING FIRE FANG!

THEN, MAGMORTAR SLAPPED BACK WITH KARATE CHOPS!

MAAAAAG-MOR-MOR-MOR-MOR!

AAA! AAA! AAA! AAA!

JUST WHEN IT SEEMED LIKE TORRACAT WAS TRAPPED, IT TURNED THE BATTLE AROUND WITH ITS BRAND-NEW ATTACK . . .

FIRST, IT KNOCKED OUT MAGMORTAR . . .
MAAAAGMOOOOOOOO!
THEN, IT FINISHED ELECTIVIRE, TOO!
CAAAAAAAAAAAAAAAT!
IIIIIIIIIIIIIRRREEEEE!
THE DOUBLE ROYALS HAD TECHNICALLY WON . . .

SO THE MASKED ROYAL AND INCINEROAR DECIDED IT WAS TIME TO USE THEIR Z-MOVE: MALICIOUS MOONSAULT.

RRRrrrRRRrrrRRRrrr
RRRrrrRRRrrrR!
KAAAAAAA...
BLAM!
ALL THE REVENGERS ARE DOWN FOR THE COUNT!
AND THE DOUBLE ROYALS ARE OUR DOUBLE WINNERS!

TOGETHER, THE MASKED ROYAL AND ASH ROYAL ACHIEVED AN EXTRAORDINARY VICTORY! THE CROWD WENT WILD—ESPECIALLY ASH'S FRIENDS.

THE DOUBLE ROYALS DID ONE LAST MOVE FOR THE FANS BEFORE STEPPING OUT OF THE RING.

BEFORE THEY PARTED WAYS, ASH THANKED THE MASKED ROYAL.
SOMEDAY, I'D LIKE YOU AND INCINEROAR TO HAVE A FINAL BATTLE WITH TORRACAT AND ME!
OF COURSE. UNTIL WE MEET AGAIN . . .
A FEW MINUTES LATER, PROFESSOR KUKUI FINALLY RETURNED WITH THOSE SNACKS . . .
SO WHAT HAVE YOU BEEN DOING THIS WHOLE TIME?!
UH . . . WELL . . . I GUESS I SORT OF GOT LOST . . .
SUDDENLY, ASH HAD A HUNCH WHERE HE MIGHT SEE THE MASKED ROYAL AGAIN . . .
TOR?!
HUH?!

Story 2:
Kahuna
Clash

ASH AND HIS POKÉMON PALS TRAVELED TO ULA'ULA ISLAND, HOPING TO CHALLENGE THE ISLAND KAHUNA, NANU, TO A GRAND TRIAL.

ASH WAS WONDERING WHEN NANU WOULD GET BACK TO THE STATION WHEN ANOTHER VISITOR LOOKING FOR NANU ARRIVED.
ALOLA!
UH, ALOLA! NANU'S NOT HERE. THE OTHER POLICE OFFICER ASKED ME TO WAIT HERE.
WAIT, THE *OTHER* POLICE OFFICER?
THERE'S ONLY ONE POLICE OFFICER WORKING HERE AT THE STATION, AND HIS NAME IS NANU.
THAT WAS NANU?!
ASH COULDN'T BELIEVE HE WAS FOOLED BY THE ISLAND KAHUNA . . .

BUT HE HOPED HE COULD TRUST HIS NEW FRIEND ACEROLA.
DON'T YOU WORRY! I'LL FIND NANU FOR YOU. HE'S A GOOD FRIEND OF MINE.

ACEROLA SHOWED ASH AND HIS POKÉMON THE ULA'ULA ISLAND LIBRARY WHILE THEY WAITED FOR NANU TO RETURN. SHE TOLD THEM A FAMOUS ALOLAN STORY.

AFTER A LOVELY AFTERNOON AT THE LIBRARY, ASH WAS GETTING ANTSY. HE WAS ABOUT TO RETURN TO THE STATION WHEN IN WALKED NANU.

THE TOY MIGHT HAVE GOTTEN NANU'S ATTENTION, BUT ASH WAS NOT HERE TO PLAY. HE HAD ONE THING ON HIS MIND—A BATTLE WITH NANU.
EXCUSE ME! I'D LIKE TO TAKE THE GRAND TRIAL FOR MY ISLAND CHALLENGE!
GO BACK TO MELEMELE ISLAND. IT'S TOO SOON FOR YOU TO HAVE A GRAND TRIAL.
JUST GIVE HIM A CHANCE!
GIVE ME A CHANCE WITH A PRE-TRIAL! WON'T YOU?
NANU THOUGHT HE COULD SCARE ASH AWAY. HE DIDN'T KNOW THAT ASH NEVER GIVES UP ON HIS GOALS!

GRRRRR!
LYCANROC, YOU'RE PSYCHED, TOO!
FINALLY, NANU DECIDED IT WOULD BE LESS ANNOYING TO BATTLE THAN TO CONTINUE TO HEAR THEM BEG.
ALL RIGHT, ALL RIGHT ALREADY.
NANU CALLED ON THE INTIMIDATION POKÉMON, KROOKODILE.
KROOOOKODILE!

WE WILL NOW BEGIN THE PRE-TRIAL BATTLE BETWEEN ASH FROM PALLET TOWN AND NANU, THE ISLAND KAHUNA OF ULA'ULA ISLAND!
ASH AND LYCANROC WERE READY TO BEGIN THE BATTLE.
LYCANROC, USE TACKLE!
GRRRRRRR!

BAM!
KROOOOOK!
GRRRRR!
LYCANROC'S POWERFUL PUSH DIDN'T BOTHER KROOKODILE. AND NEITHER DID ITS ROCK THROW BLITZ . . .
RRRRRRROC!
OR ITS FIERCE BITE.
GRRRRRR!

IT WAS ALL GOING ACCORDING TO NANU'S BATTLE PLAN . . .
EXCELLENT. NOW, MAKE IT ANGRIER!
USE SAND TOMB!
KROOOOOKAAAAAAAH!
ERRR-RRRRR-ROC!
LYCANROC!

KROOOOOOK!
CONTINUE WITH MUD-SLAP!
LYCANROC HATED BEING COVERED IN MUD, AND ITS EYES TURNED AN ANGRY RED.
GRRRR!

FILLED WITH RAGE, IT LEAPED RIGHT OUT OF THE SLIPPERY SAND.
GRRRRRRRRRRAAAA!
OH NO!
ASH TRIED TO REASON WITH HIS POKÉMON PAL . . .
PIIIIIIIIKA!
CALM DOWN, LYCANROC, PLEASE!
BUT LYCANROC IGNORED ASH AND DID WHAT IT WANTED. IT ATTACKED KROOKODILE AGAIN.
GRRRRRRR!

WELL, WELL. IT LOOKS LIKE IT'S NOT LISTENING TO YOU, IS IT, KIDDO?
NANU TOOK ADVANTAGE OF THE BREAK IN THEIR TEAMWORK.
KROOKODILE, USE COUNTER!
ALL RIGHT, USE CRUNCH!
KROOOOKODILE!
WHACK!
ARROOOO!

LYCANROC WAS LEFT UNABLE TO BATTLE. ACEROLA NAMED THE ISLAND KAHUNA THE WINNER OF THE PRE-TRIAL.
LYCANROC, ARE YOU OKAY?
TOLD YOU, KIDDO. IT'S TOO SOON TO GO FOR A GRAND TRIAL. GO BACK TO MELEMELE.
NO WAY! WE'RE GOING TO STAY RIGHT HERE AND TRAIN! AND THEN ONCE WE'RE STRONGER, WE'RE GOING TO CHALLENGE YOU AGAIN!

ASH DECIDED HE WOULD GO VISIT HIS OLD FRIEND THE ULA'ULA ISLAND GUARDIAN, TAPU BULU—A LEGENDARY POKÉMON WITH INCREDIBLE KNOWLEDGE AND POWER. PERHAPS TAPU BULU COULD HELP THEM TRAIN TO BECOME AN EVEN BETTER TEAM . . .

BUT FIRST, ASH WANTED LYCANROC TO GET A HEARTY DINNER AND A GOOD NIGHT'S REST.

THE NEXT DAY, ASH COULDN'T WAIT TO HIT THE ROAD TO VISIT TAPU BULU.

THE TERRAIN SOON TURNED FROM GREEN AND LUSH TO PURE DUST.
THIS IS THE HAINA DESERT. THE RUINS OF ABUNDANCE ARE ON THE OTHER SIDE.
NO MATTER WHICH DIRECTION YOU LOOK, IT'S ALL SAND, SAND, AND MORE SAND!
THE HAINA DESERT WASN'T JUST VERY SANDY; IT WAS ALSO VERY WINDY.
WON'T BE LONG! WE'LL BE ACROSS THE DESERT IN A JIFF.
PIIIIKAAA.
ROWLET WAS SWEPT AWAY IN A STRONG GUST, BUT LUCKILY POIPOLE CAUGHT IT.
ALL RIGHT, POIPOLE!
POIPOLE!

FINALLY, THEY ARRIVED AT A GIANT MOUNTAIN.

ASH STRUGGLED TO SCALE THE ROCK FACE, BUT HE KNEW IT WAS HIS CHANCE TO PROVE HE WAS WORTHY OF TAPU BULU'S HELP.

THE FRIENDS RACED TO THE TOP. ALTHOUGH ASH GOT THERE LAST, HE GAVE THE CLIMB HIS ALL!

THE LEGENDARY POKÉMON BARELY OPENED ITS TIRED EYES, BUT BEFORE IT COULD CLOSE THEM AGAIN, ASH AND LYCANROC ASKED THE QUESTION THEY CAME FOR.

TAPU BULU ROSE INTO THE AIR AND LIFTED ITS ARM TO REVEAL A GLOWING HOOF.
SEEDS ROLLED OUT OF THE SHINING HOOF AND TOOK ROOT IN THE GROUND.
BUUULU!
PIIIIKA?
THEN, BOTH OF TAPU BULU'S HOOFS BEGAN TO GLOW, AND IT FOCUSED ALL OF ITS MIGHT . . .
TAAAAAAAA PUUUUUUU BUUUUUUU LLUUUUUUUUU!
SOON, THE GLOW GREW . . .

AND A GIGANTIC TREE SHOT UP OUT OF THE SOIL!
TAAAAPUUU!
ASH COULDN'T BELIEVE HIS EYES!
ALL RIGHT! HOW AWESOME IS THAT?!

THE ISLAND GUARDIAN RESTED ON A BRANCH. ROTOM DEX EXPLAINED THAT TO INCREASE ITS POWER, TAPU BULU CREATES LUSH PLANTS AND THEN ABSORBS THEIR ENERGY.
BUUUULUUUUUU!
ROWLET DECIDED TO JOIN THE LEGENDARY POKÉMON AND POWER UP ON A BRANCH, TOO.
RRRRRRR!
OH!

Soon, Rowlet soared up into the sky and showed off a new attack it had never done before: Razor Leaf!

WITH ITS STRENGTH RESTORED, TAPU BULU WAS READY TO ACCEPT ASH'S TRAINING BATTLE CHALLENGE.

BUT AS A RAINSTORM BEGAN, ASH FEARED LYCANROC MIGHT NOT BE READY TO BATTLE. THE GROUND WAS WET, AND TAPU BULU PUSHED THE WOLF POKÉMON INTO THE MUD.

ROWLET AND POIPOLE TRIED TO PLAY IN THE MUD WITH THEIR PAL LYCANROC.

BUT LYCANROC BECAME FURIOUS AT ITS FRIENDS. ITS EYES TURNED FIERY RED.
IT LASHED OUT . . .
GRRRRRRRRR!
OH MAN!
PIKAAA PIKA!
RRR-RRR-RRR!

ASH KNELT DOWN BEFORE HIS BUDDY AND TRIED TO CALM IT.
BACK WHEN YOU WERE ROCKRUFF, WE USED TO PLAY IN THE RAIN LIKE THIS . . .
LYCANROC REMEMBERED . . .
WE ALWAYS HAD A LOT OF FUN. I STILL REMEMBER.
RRRRRUF!
EVEN THOUGH WE GOT ALL MUDDY, WE KEPT PLAYING.

AND THEN YOU EVOLVED, AND YOU LOOK DIFFERENT NOW THAN YOU DID BACK THEN, BUT YOU'RE STILL YOU.
YOU KNOW, I REALLY CARE ABOUT YOU, EXACTLY THE WAY YOU ARE!
SUDDENLY, THE RAIN CLOUDS DISAPPEARED. THE SUN RETURNED . . . AND SO DID LYCANROC.
YOU'RE THE BEST. I COULDN'T BE MORE PROUD OF YOU!

Everyone was happy to see that Lycanroc was feeling better and ready to train! Tapu Bulu rose back into the sky.

Tapu Bulu began the battle by covering the field in Grassy Terrain.

HERE WE GO! LET'S GIVE IT EVERYTHING WE'VE GOT!
TAPU BULU SWUNG INTO ACTION WITH WOOD HAMMER!
BULUUUU!
LYCANROC TOOK A HIT AND SLAMMED STRAIGHT INTO THE FACE OF THE MOUNTAIN.
ROOC!

BUT IT GOT BACK UP, READY FOR MORE BATTLE, AND RESPONDED WITH A RAIN OF ROCK THROW.
GRRRRRR!
TAPU BULU SWOOPED UP INTO THE AIR, AND ITS HORNS BEGAN TO GLOW.
TAPU BULU'S USING HORN LEECH!
THEN, IT PREPARED A DOUBLE PUNCH OF SOLAR BEAM.
BUUUUULLLLLUUUUUU!

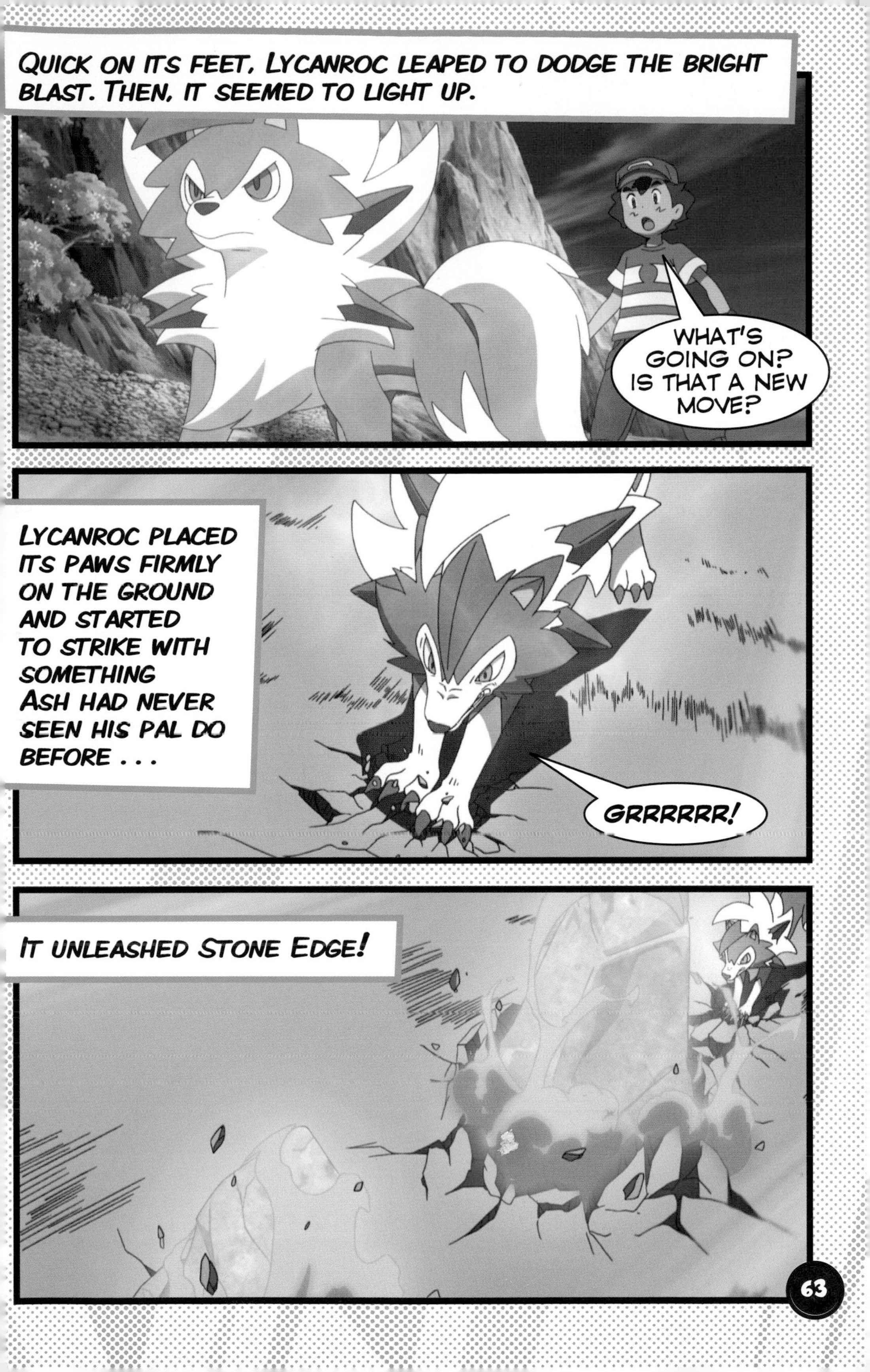
QUICK ON ITS FEET, LYCANROC LEAPED TO DODGE THE BRIGHT BLAST. THEN, IT SEEMED TO LIGHT UP.
WHAT'S GOING ON? IS THAT A NEW MOVE?
LYCANROC PLACED ITS PAWS FIRMLY ON THE GROUND AND STARTED TO STRIKE WITH SOMETHING ASH HAD NEVER SEEN HIS PAL DO BEFORE . . .
GRRRRRR!
IT UNLEASHED STONE EDGE!

Big boulders shot up from the ground and went straight from Lycanroc to Tapu Bulu. Tapu Bulu tried to shield itself from the boulders . . .

But Stone Edge shot it toward the mountainside.

Suddenly, the powerful Legendary Pokémon stopped itself in midair, just shy of hitting the rock face. It began to clap its hoofs and ring its bell.

THEN, TAPU BULU SPUN AROUND THE GIANT TREE, MAKING IT GLOW AGAIN. SOON, BIG BLUE ORAN BERRIES APPEARED ON ITS BRANCHES.

THE ISLAND GUARDIAN PICKED A DELICIOUS BERRY FOR EVERYONE.

Now Ash and Lycanroc felt ready to return and challenge Nanu. So they said their good-byes to the awesome Island Guardian and hit the road.

Meanwhile, some familiar faces had journeyed to Ula'ula Island looking to battle Ash—Team Rocket.

TEAM ROCKET HAD BEEN HELD CAPTIVE ON THE ISLAND BY A CONTROLLING BEWEAR WHO LOVED THEM TOO MUCH.

BUT THEY CLEVERLY CREATED TALKING ROBOTS TO FOOL BEWEAR AND MAKE IT THINK THEY WERE STILL THERE.

FREE TO MAKE TROUBLE AGAIN, TEAM ROCKET WENT LOOKING FOR ASH AT THE LOCAL POLICE STATION.

QUESTION! YOU *DO* KNOW WHERE THE TWERP IS, DON'T YOU? HE'S GOT A PIKACHU AND A LYCANROC.

YOU MEAN THAT KID FROM PALLET TOWN? HE'S HERE.

BUT WHERE IS HERE?

UH . . . AT THE ABANDONED THRIFTY MEGA MART.

MIMIKYU COULDN'T WAIT FOR ITS CHANCE TO USE ITS NEW Z-MOVE ON ITS RIVAL PIKACHU.
HISSSS HISSSSSSS!
MIMIKYU, YOU LOOK LIKE YOU'RE GONNA BLOW A GASKET!
SO TEAM ROCKET RACED TOWARD THE ABANDONED THRIFTY MEGA MART TO FIND ASH AND FINALLY CATCH PIKACHU.
BUT THEY DON'T KNOW THAT NANU WAS SO LAZY, HE MADE UP ASH'S LOCATION! AND SOON AFTER TEAM ROCKET LEFT THE STATION, ASH ARRIVED TO CHALLENGE NANU.
LYCANROC'S A LOT STRONGER NOW! I'D LIKE A REMATCH, PLEASE.
AS IF DEALING WITH *THEM* FIRST WASN'T BAD ENOUGH, NOW YOU WANT A REMATCH . . .
IF YOU HAD TO DEAL WITH *THEM* FIRST—WAIT, WHO ARE THEY?

THEY ARE THESE GUYS WHO REALLY WANT TO BATTLE WITH YOU, KIDDO . . . WAIT, I'VE GOT IT! YOU CAN RETAKE THE PRE-TRIAL.
OH, YEAH! ALL RIGHT! WE'LL DO GREAT, LYCANROC! SO WHAT KIND OF PRE-TRIAL IS IT?
THERE'S A TRAINER WITH A MIMIKYU IN TOW WHERE THE THRIFTY MEGA MART USED TO BE. BEAT THAT TRAINER IN A BATTLE. HOW SIMPLE COULD IT BE?
ASH HAD NO IDEA NANU WAS TALKING ABOUT THE BAD TROOP ASH HAD BEEN BATTLING SINCE BACK IN KANTO—TEAM ROCKET.

ALL RIGHT! BRING IT ON!

WITH HIS FRIENDS BY HIS SIDE, ASH SET OUT FOR HIS PRE-TRIAL REMATCH AT THE ABANDONED MEGA MART! BUT TEAM ROCKET HAD ALREADY ARRIVED AT THE DARK, EMPTY STORE. IT WAS SO SCARY, MEOWTH THOUGHT HE SAW A GHOST.

THEN TEAM ROCKET HEARD THE SQUEAKY WHEELS OF A SHOPPING CART ROLLING THEIR WAY. COULD IT BE ANOTHER GHOST?!

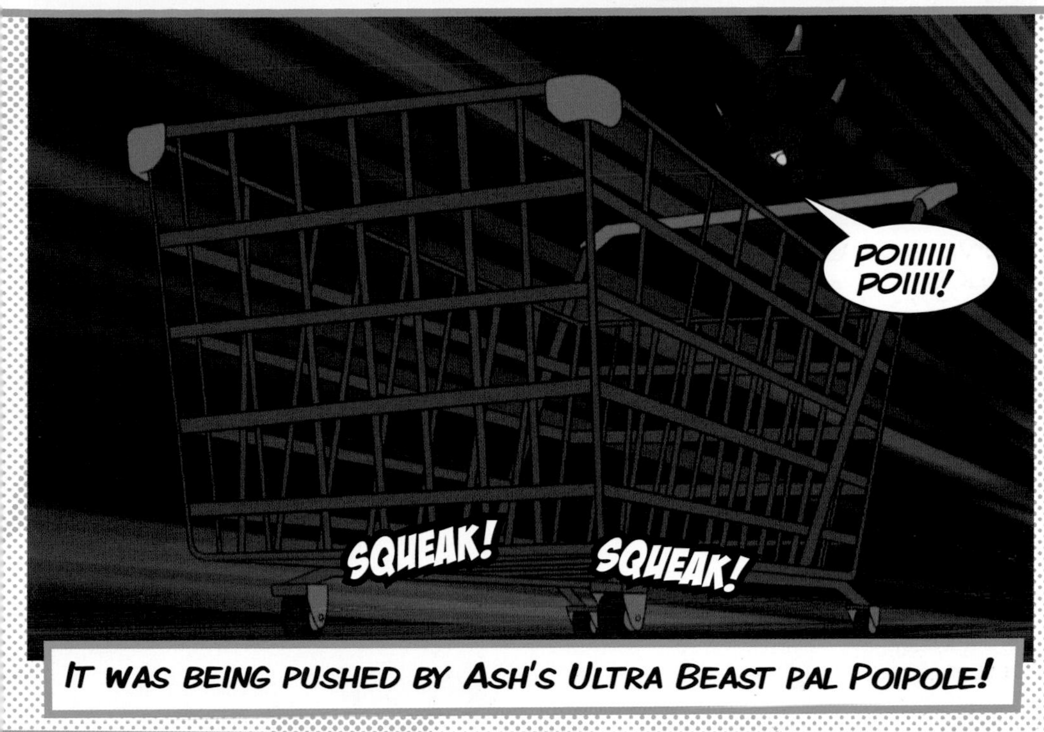

IT WAS BEING PUSHED BY ASH'S ULTRA BEAST PAL POIPOLE!

NEXT, IT WAS ASH'S TURN TO BE FREAKED OUT WHEN HE ARRIVED ON THE SCENE TO SEE JESSIE, JAMES, MEOWTH, WOBBUFFET, AND MIMIKYU READY TO FIGHT!

HUH?
TEAM ROCKET?! DOES THAT MEAN YOU'RE THE ONES I'M SUPPOSED TO HAVE MY PRE-TRIAL WITH? AND YOUR MIMIKYU?!
OH!
CLUELESS AS USUAL. WE'LL WIPE THE GROCERY STORE FLOOR WITH YOU! TODAY'S THE DAY WE TAKE POSSESSION OF YOUR PIKACHU!
I ACCEPT YOUR CHALLENGE! PIKACHU, LET'S DO IT!
PIKA PIKA!

ALL RIGHT. BATTLE BEGIN!
ALL RIGHT, PIKACHU. IRON TAIL!
PIIIIKAAAA!
PIKACHU LANDED A TOUGH IRON TAIL RIGHT ON MIMIKYU'S HEAD, BUT IT DIDN'T EVEN FLINCH.
HISSSSSSS!
THEN, MIMIKYU LANDED A SHADOW CLAW SLAP.

PIKACHU THREW A FIERCE ELECTRO BALL, BUT MIMIKYU TREATED IT MORE LIKE A BASEBALL. IT USED WOOD HAMMER LIKE A BAT TO HIT IT RIGHT BACK.

ASH ASKED PIKACHU TO TRY THUNDERBOLT.
PIIIIIIIIKKKKKAAAAAA . . .
POI POIPOLE!

BUT BEFORE PIKACHU COULD FIRE ITS FAMOUS ZAP, MIMIKYU KNOCKED IT OUT OF THE AIR WITH ANOTHER SHADOW CLAW CLAP.
HISSSS!
PIKACHU!

EVEN TEAM ROCKET COULDN'T BELIEVE THAT IT WAS LOOKING LIKE THEY'D WIN THIS BATTLE THANKS TO SUPER STRONG MIMIKYU . . .
TIME TO WRAP THIS BABY UP!
MIMIKYU! LET'S FINISH THIS WITH OUR Z-MOVE!
WOOOBBUFFET!

But as Team Rocket tried to snap into action, they were interrupted by a very big, and very upset, Bewear.
AAAAAAAAAHHHHH!

Bewear had figured out that Team Rocket had tricked it with robots and run away.
THAAATTT IS MEEEOOWTH FOR YOOOU.

Bewear was so annoyed that it traveled all the way across Ula'ula Island to take Team Rocket back.
FANCY MEETING YOU HERE . . .
BEWARE THE BEWEAR . . .
HA HA HA . . .

SUDDENLY, BEWEAR PUT TEAM ROCKET DOWN AND SAT PATIENTLY.

IT SEEMED MIMIKYU COULD EVEN SCARE BEWEAR!

MIMIKYU WAS READY TO GET BACK TO THE BATTLE—
AND IT WAS DOUBLE THE TROUBLE!
PIKACHU, HEADS UP!
HISS, HISSSSSS!
THE DISGUISE POKÉMON WHIPPED
TWO WALLOPS OF SHADOW CLAW.
NOW, USE IRON TAIL!

BUT PIKACHU WASN'T GOING TO GIVE UP! IT BROKE AWAY AND STARTED TO SWIPE ITS IRON TAIL AT MIMIKYU LIKE A SWORD.

PIKACHU RACED ACROSS THE STORE, TRYING TO BUY SOME TIME FOR STRATEGY. BUT MIMIKYU CHASED IT AROUND EVERY CORNER. IT WAS TOO FAST AND TOO FURIOUS!

ASH MOTIVATED HIS BEST FRIEND TO KEEP UP THE FIGHT . . .

PIKACHU POWERED UP ANOTHER AMAZING ELECTRO BALL.

BUT MIMIKYU WHACKED IT AWAY WITH ANOTHER WOOD HAMMER.

NOW PIKACHU WAS WORN OUT, AND IT TRIED TO CATCH ITS BREATH.

PLEASE, PIKACHU, GET UP! MIMIKYU'S GOING TO USE A Z-MOVE NOW . . .
COME ON! YOU CAN DO IT!
PI PI PIKA . . .
READY!

JESSIE FLASHED HER Z-RING WITH HER Z-CRYSTAL, DARKINIUM Z.

STRAIGHT FROM THE HEART!
WOOOOBBA WOBBAH!
WOBBUFFET!
TA-DA!

IT SAYS THE MOVE'S NAME IS "LET'S SNUGGLE FOREVER."
A BIT LONG, BUT WHY NOT?
LET'S SNUGGLE FOREVER!
WOBBA WOBBAAA!
MIMIKYU SCOOTED ACROSS THE FLOOR AS IT PREPARED TO UNLEASH ITS Z-MOVE.
HISSSSSSSS!

PIKACHU MUSTERED ITS STRENGTH AND FOUGHT BACK WITH A BIG ELECTRO BALL!
PIIIIIKKKAAAA!
THEN MIMIKYU SMOTHERED THE ELECTRO BALL UNDER ITS CLOAK WITH ITS Z-MOVE!
BUT IT SEEMED THE BATTLE WAS CONTINUING UNDER THE CLOAK . . .

PIKA PIKAAAA!
HISS HISS HISS HISS!
PLEASE HANG IN THERE, PIKACHU!

THAT MOVE WILL CURL YOUR NOSE HAIRS . . . LET'S SNUGGLE FOREVER IS SCARY!
EEEEEEEEH!
AAAACKKKK!
WHEN MIMIKYU MOVED, THEY ALL SAW A LIGHT . . .
YOU'RE OKAY, PIKACHU!
IT'S ELECTROWEB! PIKACHU PROTECTED ITSELF BY USING IT AS A SHIELD!
POI POLE!
SO COOL, PIKACHU! YOU LEARNED HOW TO USE ELECTROWEB! LET'S GIVE IT ONE MORE SHOT. ELECTROWEB, AGAIN!

PIKACHU JUMPED INTO ACTION, SPINNING ANOTHER SUPERCHARGED ELECTROWEB!
PIKA PIKA PIIIKACHUUUUUU!
MIMIKYU TRIED TO SHRED ELECTROWEB WITH SPEEDY SWINGS OF WOOD HAMMER BUT SOON FOUND ITSELF COMPLETELY TRAPPED.
BUZZZZ
HIIIIISSSSSSS!

RIGHT BEFORE HIS EYES, ASH'S Z-CRYSTAL CHANGED FROM A DIAMOND TO A LIGHTNING BOLT.

MUCH BIGGER THAN A THUNDERBOLT . . .
PIIIKA!
YEAH, THIS IS MUCH, MUCH BIGGER! AT SUPER-FULL POWER!
PIKA PIKAAA!

PIKACHU! USE TEN MILLION VOLT THUNDERBOLT!
PIIKAAAAAAAAAAAA!
PI-KA, PI-KA, PI-KA . . .
CHUUUUUUUUUUUUU!

PIKACHU AND ASH'S Z-MOVE WAS SO STRONG, IT BLEW THE ROOF OFF THE MEGA MART AND SHOT A BEAM OF LIGHT STRAIGHT INTO THE SKY! BUT MOST IMPORTANT, IT DEFEATED MIGHTY MIMIKYU.

THEN, BEWEAR FILLED ITS SHOPPING CART AND HEADED HOME.

REFEREE ACEROLA OFFICIALLY DECLARED ASH THE WINNER!
ALL RIGHT! WE WON, BUDDY!
POIPOLE!
IN THE PARKING LOT, THE CELEBRATION CONTINUED AS THEY RAN INTO THE ISLAND KAHUNA.
A PROMISE IS A PROMISE. GRAND TRIAL— YOU'RE ON, KID!
YEAH! THANK YOU SO MUCH! OKAY, GRAND TRIAL. I'M READY!

As Ash headed to the Ruins of Abundance, he was so excited to start his third grand trial . . . and it seemed Nanu was excited about it, too, even if he didn't want to admit it.
You actually act like an island kahuna whenever there's a grand trial.
It wears me out coming all the way here to the ruins, I'll tell you . . . but it's not so bad once in a while.
Let's get this show on the road.
Acerola volunteered to be the referee. Nanu began with the rules of the battle.
In order to pass the Ula'ula Island Grand Trial, you must defeat all three of my Pokémon.
Here's the catch . . . you must do it with only one Pokémon, kiddo!

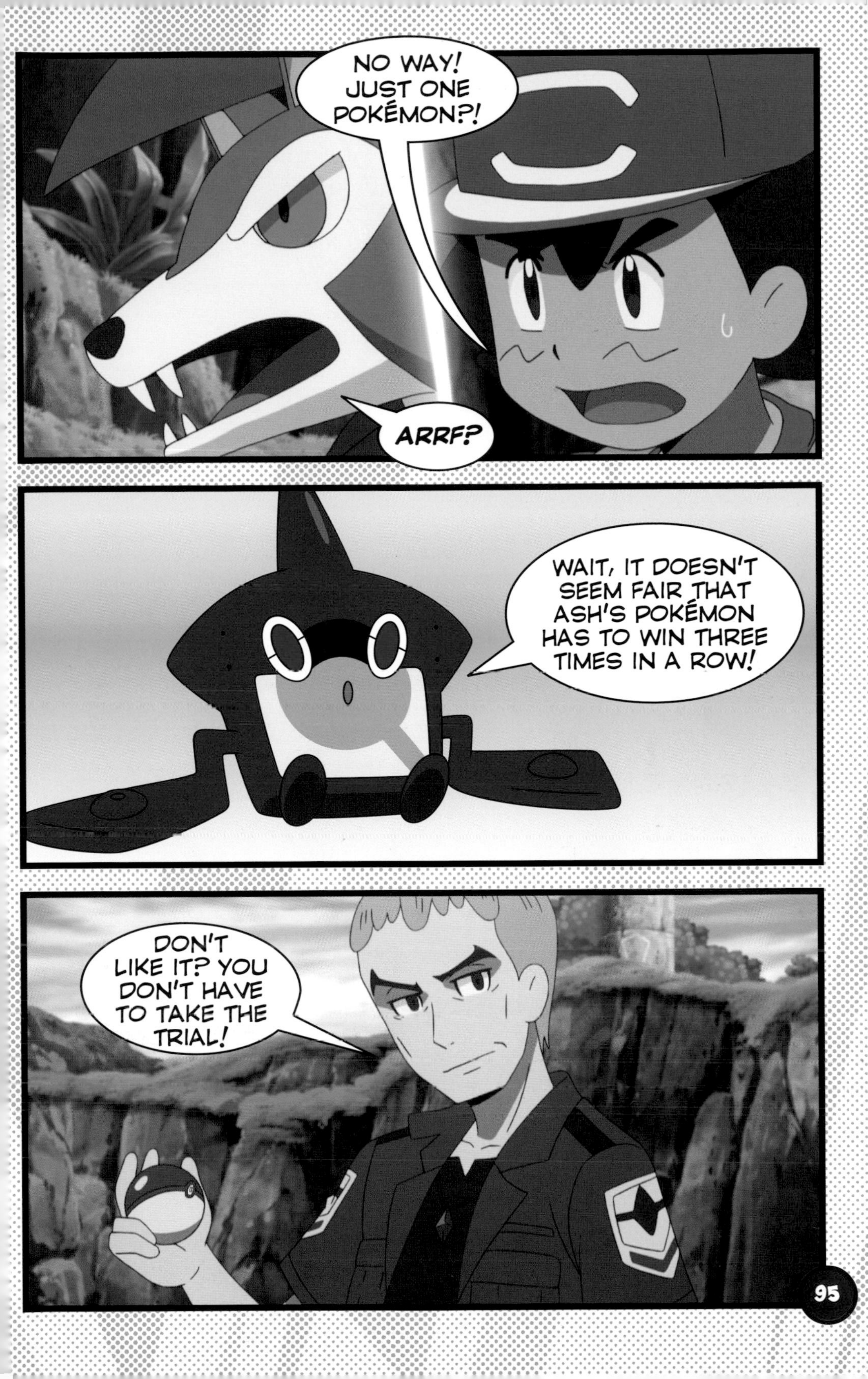
NO WAY! JUST ONE POKÉMON?!
ARRF?
WAIT, IT DOESN'T SEEM FAIR THAT ASH'S POKÉMON HAS TO WIN THREE TIMES IN A ROW!
DON'T LIKE IT? YOU DON'T HAVE TO TAKE THE TRIAL!

ASH HAD MADE IT THIS FAR, SO HE WANTED TO KEEP GOING. BUT FIRST, HE HAD TO ASK LYCANROC.
LOOKS LIKE THE BATTLE IS GOING TO BE TOUGH. ARE YOU UP FOR IT?
LYCANROC!
THEN WE ACCEPT!
I HOPE YOU TRAINED. YOU'LL NEED IT!

NANU TOSSED HIS FIRST POKÉ BALL . . .
KROOOOKAH!
IT'S KROOKODILE!
KROOKODILE HAD ALREADY DEFEATED LYCANROC ONCE. AND NOW . . .
I'LL MAKE THE FIRST MOVE!
IT'S USING ITS SPECIAL ABILITY TO INTIMIDATE LYCANROC!

KROOKODILE TRAPPED LYCANROC IN SINKING SAND TOMB AND THEN PELTED IT WITH MUD-SLAP.

BUT LYCANROC REMEMBERED ALL OF ITS SPECIAL TRAINING WITH TAPU BULU AND STAYED STRONG. EVEN THOUGH ITS EYES TURNED RED, IT KEPT ITS COOL, AND THEY RETURNED TO GREEN.

NANU WAS IMPRESSED TO SEE LYCANROC'S NEWFOUND STRENGTH.

LYCANROC SHOWERED KROOKODILE IN A ROCK THROW HAIL.
ARRRRRRRRRRRRRR!
BUT KROOKODILE USED COUNTER TO SWAT THE STONES AWAY WITH ITS TAIL.
CAN'T YOU SEE IT'S USELESS?
KROOK KROOK KROOK!
NEXT, KROOKODILE TRIED A CLOSE-RANGE ATTACK WITH A BIG BITE—CRUNCH!
KROO-O-KODIIILE!
DODGE IT!
RRROC!

ASH ASKED LYCANROC TO AGAIN USE ROCK THROW, BUT KROOKODILE AGAIN STOPPED IT WITH COUNTER.

THIS IS CERTAINLY GETTING TO BE A BORE. I GUESS I OVERESTIMATED YOU, ASH. ISN'T THE ESSENCE OF A POKÉMON BATTLE THE ACT OF PITTING YOUR BEST ATTACK AGAINST SOMEONE ELSE'S?

LYCANROC WAS READY TO SHUT OUT KROOKODILE AND SHUT NANU UP! IT HUDDLED WITH ASH AND CAME UP WITH A PLAN.

LYCANROC SPED STRAIGHT FOR KROOKODILE, WHICH PREPARED TO PROTECT ITSELF WITH COUNTER . . .

THEN LYCANROC SURPRISED KROOKODILE WITH ANOTHER BLAST OF BOULDERS!
GET IT IN ONE SHOT! USE ROCK THROW!
ARRRROOOOOO!
KROO-KA?!
WITH THAT, KROOKODILE WAS LEFT UNABLE TO BATTLE.
LYCANROC WAS DECLARED THE WINNER OF THE FIRST ROUND!
YOU DID IT, LYCANROC!
RAWR!
THAT MAKES ASH AND LYCANROC'S FIRST WIN!
HE HE HE!

YOU REALLY WEREN'T HALF BAD!
I DIDN'T MEAN YOU, KIDDO. I WAS TALKING TO LYCANROC!
IT DOESN'T MATTER. THANKS A LOT.
FOR WHAT?
FOR SAYING THAT A POKÉMON BATTLE IS ABOUT YOUR BEST MOVES GOING HEAD-TO-HEAD WITH EACH OTHER.
THAT'S JUST HOW I LIKE TO BATTLE!

NANU WAS READY FOR LESS CHITCHAT AND MORE BATTLE! HE CALLED ON HIS SECOND POKÉMON PAL.
HERE WE GO!
YOUR NEXT OPPONENT IS SABLEYE!
RRRRRR!
SABLEYE DIDN'T WASTE A SECOND. IT STARTED THE BATTLE WITH SHADOW BALL.
SAAAAAAY-BULLLLL-EEEEEYE!

LYCANROC WAS READY FOR IT!
ARRRROOOOO!
SABLEYE THEN SENT A SLY ATTACK TO GO BEHIND LYCANROC'S BACK.
SHADOW SNEAK!
EYYYYECK!
ARRRRRO?!
LYCANROC, NOOOO!
LYCANROC DIDN'T SEE IT COMING, AND THE SHADOW LANDED A SMACK.

BEFORE LYCANROC COULD MAKE ANOTHER MOVE, IT GOT STUNNED BY SABLEYE'S MEAN LOOK!

LYCANROC WAS COMPLETELY FROZEN WITH FEAR.
LYCANROC GOT THE FULL BRUNT OF MEAN LOOK! IT CAN'T MOVE!
RA-AH-AH-ACK!
NANU SEIZED THE MOMENT.
NOW, A SERIES OF SHADOW CLAW ATTACKS!
SABLEYE SABLE!

Ash wasn't going to let his friend Lycanroc just sit there and get scratched. He thought fast and had the Wolf Pokémon Bite back!

Lycanroc tried with all its might . . . but it just couldn't move close enough to Sableye to strike it.

The shadow slapped the trapped Lycanroc back and forth . . .

The Wolf Pokémon tried to stay strong!

AS SABLEYE WENT TO USE SHADOW CLAW, LYCANROC'S EYES TURNED BRIGHT RED. THIS WORRIED ASH MORE THAN THE ATTACKS . . .
SABLE SABLE SABLEYYYYYE!
RRRRRRRRRRRR!
NO, LYCANROC! KEEP YOUR COOL!
DETERMINED, LYCANROC WAS ABLE TO DODGE SABLEYE'S SWIPES!
BUT EVEN MORE SHOCKING, NANU SHARED SOME ADVICE WITH ASH.
LOOK CLOSELY, KIDDO. SEE WHAT'S GOING ON?
MAYBE WHEN YOUR LYCANROC GETS ANGRY WITH THOSE RED EYES, IT ACTUALLY GETS STRONGER.
BUT WHEN IT GETS ANGRY, IT CAN'T HEAR ME AT ALL.
ARE YOU SURE ABOUT THAT?

ASH PAUSED TO THINK, BUT NANU KEPT GOING.
WHATEVER. SABLEYE, WRAP IT UP WITH SHADOW CLAW!
THEN, ASH CALLED OUT TO HIS WOLF POKÉMON PAL . . .
LYCANROC, USE STONE EDGE!

LYCANROC LISTENED TO ASH AND DUG ITS CLAWS INTO THE BATTLEFIELD . . .
RRRRAAAAAAAA RRRAWR!
AND SUDDENLY, BIG BOULDERS AMBUSHED SABLEYE.
BOOM!
SAAABLE SAAAAABBBBLLLLEEEEEEEYE!

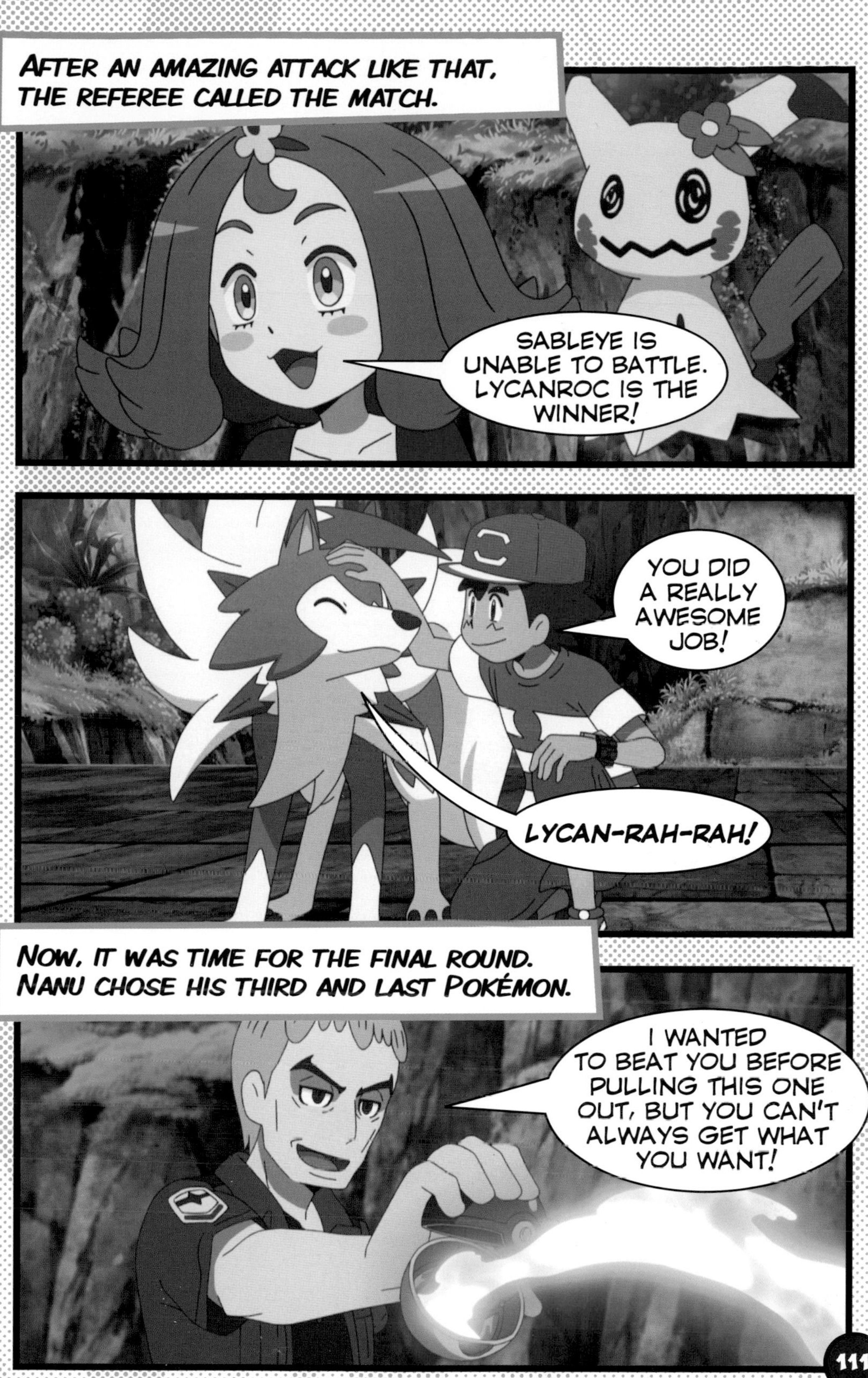
After an amazing attack like that, the referee called the match.
SABLEYE IS UNABLE TO BATTLE. LYCANROC IS THE WINNER!
YOU DID A REALLY AWESOME JOB!
LYCAN-RAH-RAH!
Now, it was time for the final round. Nanu chose his third and last Pokémon.
I WANTED TO BEAT YOU BEFORE PULLING THIS ONE OUT, BUT YOU CAN'T ALWAYS GET WHAT YOU WANT!

A NEW CHALLENGER ARRIVED ON THE BATTLEFIELD: ALOLAN PERSIAN.
HANG IN THERE, LYCANROC!
ROC!
STONE EDGE, LET'S GO!
LYCANROC USED ITS SUPER STRONG STONE EDGE AGAIN. IT KNOCKED ALOLAN PERSIAN OFF ITS FEET, BUT IT GOT RIGHT BACK UP AS IF NOTHING HAPPENED.
PERRRR!

YOU'VE REALLY BEEN TRAINING. GOOD, KIDDO.
BUT I MUST SAY, EVEN IF YOU WEREN'T HERE, LYCANROC WOULD BE JUST FINE.
NOT ONLY THAT, BUT I THINK LYCANROC MIGHT DO BETTER WITHOUT YOU.
I'M SIMPLY TELLING YOU LIKE IT IS. A POKÉMON SHOULD CHOOSE THE TRAINER BEST SUITED FOR THEM.
ARE YOU SAYING I'M NOT? WE'VE BEEN TOGETHER EVER SINCE IT WAS A ROCKRUFF! AND EVER SINCE, IT'S BEEN DOING ITS BEST! IT EVEN EVOLVED! GET IT?!

THERE! YOU SEE? THAT TEMPER OF YOURS IS THE ABSOLUTE WORST. WHY, YOU COULD BE THE POSTER CHILD FOR BAD TRAINERS.
NOW YOU'VE DONE IT!
ASH WAS SO ENRAGED THAT HE FELL RIGHT INTO NANU'S TRAP.
JUST HOW I WANT YOU.

While Ash was distracted, Nanu had Persian strike with an attack.
All right, Persian. Use Dark Pulse!
AAAAAAAAH!
Because Ash didn't have his head in the game, Lycanroc took a direct hit.
RRRROOOOOOOOOOOOCK!
Lycanroc! You've got to shake it off!

ASH QUICKLY ASKED LYCANROC TO USE ACCELEROCK, BUT THE ATTACK WAS STOPPED WITH ANOTHER DARK PULSE FROM PERSIAN. NANU TOOK THE OPPORTUNITY TO COACH LYCANROC.

BUT THE MINUTE LYCANROC WAS READY, NANU HAD PERSIAN SEND YET ANOTHER DARK PULSE PUNCH.

AND LYCANROC TOOK ANOTHER DIRECT HIT.

WHY DO YOU KEEP USING THE SAME MOVE?
SEE FOR YOURSELF . . . I LIKE THE LOOK IN ITS EYES.
SO YOU WERE JUST TRYING TO MAKE IT MAD?!
OF COURSE—THEN IT WON'T FOLLOW ORDERS ANYMORE. THE TWO OF YOU SELF-DESTRUCTING IS THE BEST END RESULT FOR ME.
WE'LL NEVER EVER DO THAT!
CHILL OUT, LYCANROC! YOU'VE GOT TO GET A HOLD OF YOURSELF!

ASH COULD SEE THAT LYCANROC WAS IN A FRENZY FROM NANU'S BULLYING AND ALOLAN PERSIAN'S BLOWS. BUT ITS NEXT ATTACK SEEMED EVEN CRAZIER!

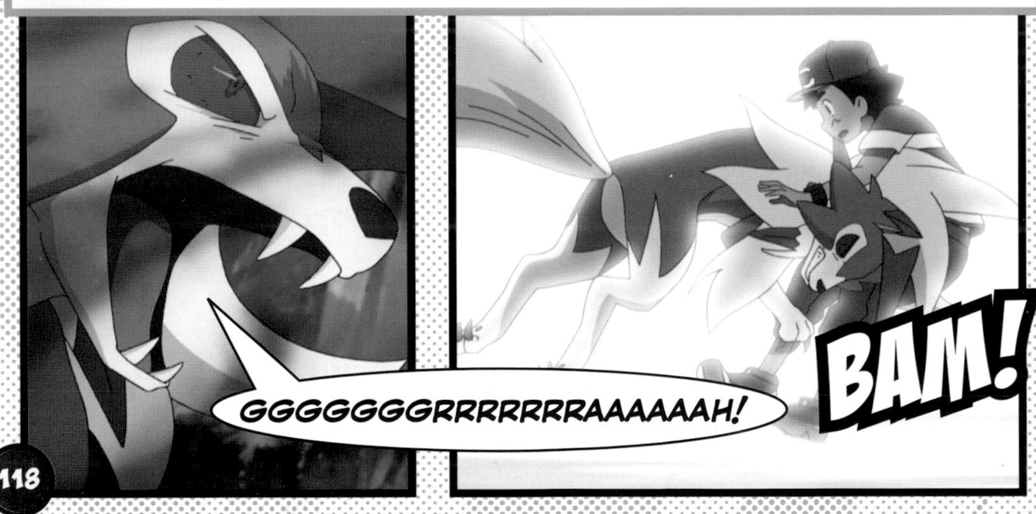

GETTING KNOCKED DOWN ALSO KNOCKED SOME SENSE INTO ASH. SUDDENLY, HE REALIZED WHAT WAS BEHIND LYCANROC'S RED EYES . . .

YOU'VE BEEN ABLE TO CONTROL IT FOR A WHILE NOW . . .
I'M SORRY! I DIDN'T REALIZE.
AND HERE I'VE BEEN A TOTAL IDIOT FOR LETTING NANU'S WORDS GET TO ME. YOU KNOW, TACKLING ME LIKE THAT DID THE TRICK.
RRRRRROC!
NOW, BACK TO THE BATTLE!
RRROC!

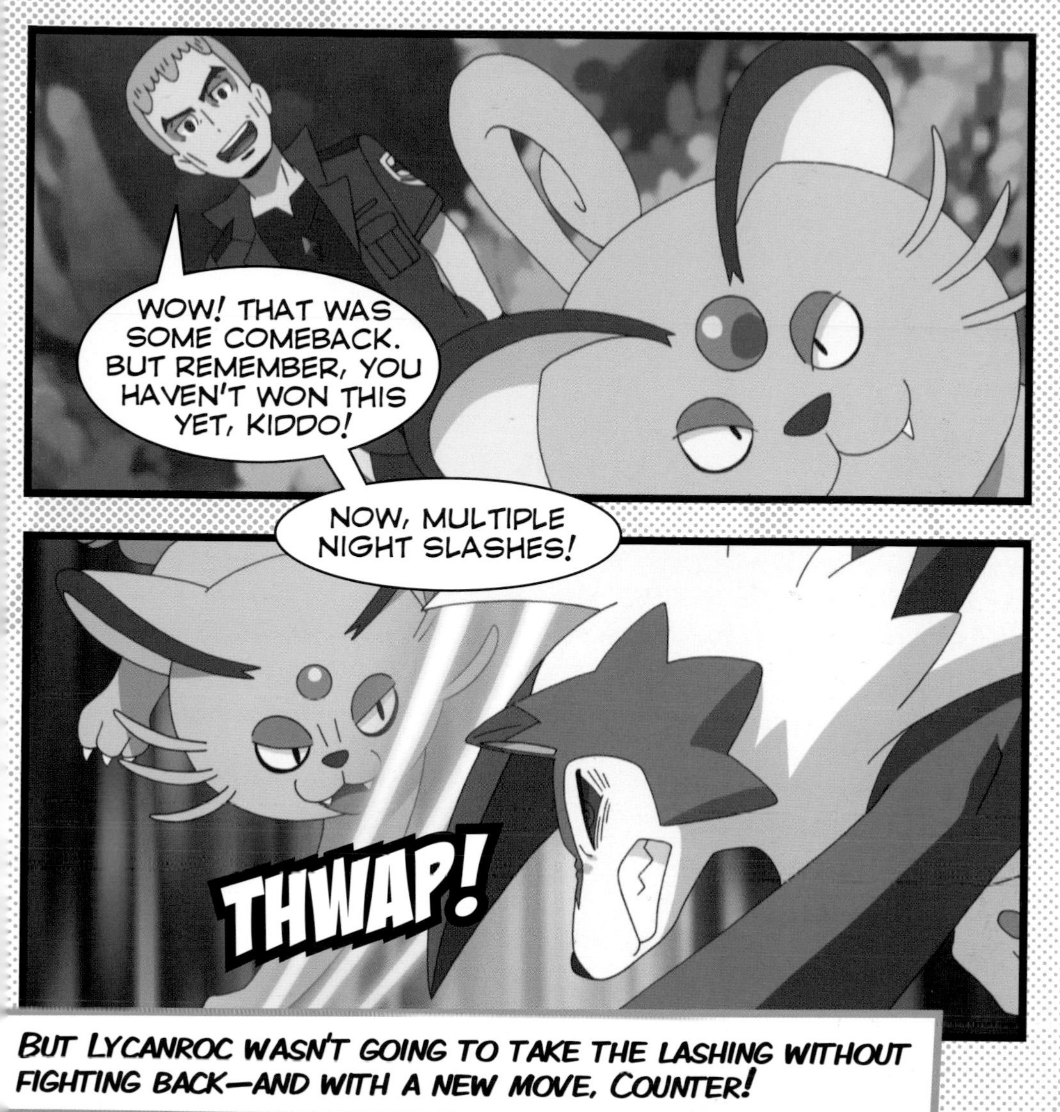

BUT LYCANROC WASN'T GOING TO TAKE THE LASHING WITHOUT FIGHTING BACK—AND WITH A NEW MOVE, COUNTER!

NANU KNEW HE WAS GOING TO HAVE TO BRING IT IF HE WAS GOING TO WIN THIS BATTLE AGAINST ASH AND LYCANROC. SO HE SNAPPED HIS Z-CRYSTAL INTO HIS Z-RING TO BEGIN A Z-MOVE!

IIIIIIAAAAAAAAAAAH!
A Z-MOVE FOR A Z-MOVE!
RRRRRR!
ALL RIGHT, LYCANROC! NOW, HERE WE GO . . .

ARRRRRRRRRRRRRAWR!
CONTINENTAL CRUSH!
FULL POWER, NOW!
RRRRRAAAOOOOOOOOOOOO!

Lycanroc blasted a giant globe of rocks right at Alolan Persian's Black Hole Eclipse.
KA-BOOM!

THE TWO Z-MOVES EXPLODED IN MIDAIR AND CANCELED EACH OTHER OUT.
AS ROCKS FROM CONTINENTAL CRUSH RAINED DOWN ON THE BATTLEFIELD, ASH DECIDED TO ADD ONE MORE ATTACK WHILE NANU WAS DISTRACTED . . .
NOW, USE ACCELEROCK!
RRRRRRRRRRRROC!
IIIIIIAAAAAAAA!
WHAM!
WITH LYCANROC'S AWESOME TACKLE, ALOLAN PERSIAN WAS LEFT UNABLE TO BATTLE.
THANKS TO HIS BOLD BUDDY LYCANROC, ASH HAD WON HIS GRAND TRIAL ON ULA'ULA ISLAND!
WELL DONE, KID.
THANK YOU VERY MUCH!

NANU AWARDED ASH HIS PRECIOUS PRIZE.
AND YOU'VE EARNED A DARK-TYPE Z-CRYSTAL WITH YOUR WIN.
BUT YOU'RE NOT SUITED TO THE DARK, ARE YOU, KIDDO?
SO INSTEAD, A LYCANIUM Z.
WHAT'S THAT?
A Z-CRYSTAL THAT CAN ONLY BE USED TO LAUNCH A Z-MOVE WITH LYCANROC.
OH WOW, LYCANIUM Z!

ASH WAS HAPPY HE WAS VICTORIOUS BUT SAD TO SAY GOOD-BYE TO ULA'ULA ISLAND. AS THE FERRY PULLED OUT OF THE DOCK, HE FELT SO GRATEFUL FOR ALL THE TERRIFIC TIMES, TOUGH TRAINING, AND EVEN TOUGHER BATTLES HE FACED THERE.
THANKS SO MUCH!
BE SURE TO COME SEE US ON ULA'ULA ISLAND AGAIN!
THAT BATTLE REALLY LOOKED LIKE A LOT OF FUN.
YOU KNOW, I'D NEVER MISS A GRAND TRIAL THAT FORCES ME TO GIVE 100 PERCENT.
THAT'S FOR SURE!
AS ULA'ULA ISLAND FADED ON THE HORIZON, ASH SET HIS SIGHTS ON HIS NEXT BIG BATTLE . . .
LET'S KEEP GETTING STRONGER, AND THEN WE CAN BE SURE WE PASS THE NEXT GRAND TRIAL!
PIKACHU!
POIPOLE!
ROC!